GW00402176

Winners All

*Winners
of the
1996 Brian Moore
Short Story Competition*

Limited Edition of 500

No. 464

Preface by Maeve Binchy

ADARE PRESS
White Gables
Ballymoney Hill
Banbridge
Telephone: 018206 - 23782

© 1997 Marilyn McLaughlin, Philip McClean,
Irene Maxwell, Simon Kerr,
Michael Smyth, Eileen Patterson,
Anne Harris, Liz Hansford, and Peter Dougherty.
Published by Adare Press
Typeset & Printed by Banbridge Chronicle Press Ltd.

All rights reserved. No part of this publication
may be reproduced, stored in a retrieval system,
or transmitted, in any form or by any means,
electronic, mechanical, photocopying, recording
or otherwise, without the prior permission in
writing, of the publisher.

ISBN 1-899496-08-4

The following is a list of all those who supported the 1996 Brian Moore Short Story Awards. The Creative Writers' Network thanks each and every one.

Belfast Telegraph

The Arts Council of N. Ireland

Verbal Arts Centre

Waterstone's

Blackstaff Press Ltd

Adare Press

Maeve Binchy

A. T. & General Workers' Union

Community Arts Forum

Dillon's

MacMillan Publishers

Banbridge Chronicle Press Ltd

Preface

I don't know when I enjoyed anything as much as judging the twenty short stories in the Brian Moore Competition.

First - it was a competition in honour of a writer whom I admire and know. It was good to be associated with it.

Second - it was set up by the Creative Writers' Network an organisation which does great work encouraging the spark and hope that lies within every Irish person in the belief that we can tell a story. Without this kind of scaffolding how many of us might not dare to write words and let others read them? We are all basically cowardly and fearful in case people might think we are showing off.

I read these twenty stories over a long weekend and I was taken away into twenty different worlds of imagination. I wish there were space for them all to be included in the anthology but you will greatly enjoy "The West" by Marilyn McLaughlin and "Man and Wife" by Philip McClean.

Congratulations to everyone involved and continued success and enthusiasm to all the creative writers who abound in this country.

Maeve Binchy

Contents

The West

by Marilyn McLaughlin

Granny was always odd, they said. And that's why they sent me there, because, being odd herself, she doesn't notice it in others, and was likely to put up with me better than they could at that time. They hoped you see, for me to get better, to change back into what they wanted. So it didn't make sense to me, from their point of view, to send me off to stay with someone odd. But then, they don't have much sense. Perhaps they think two oddities cancel each other out. Anyway, the doctor said that I needed space free from conflict and confrontation, real or imaginary. I needed time to heal my psychic wounds, real or imaginary. The doctor made it up as he went along. I could tell by his eyes. But they of course, believe every word spoken by a doctor, lawyer, teacher or anyone at all on TV and Radio 4.

My body, previously a flat, uninhabited plain was developing a new geography. I didn't like this. I was getting soft zones. I could feel garlands of flesh begin to settle around my waist and shoulders. I hated this. It weighed me down. Mum said that I will inherit a full and graceful female figure, and should celebrate. But she would say that wouldn't she? Look at *her*. Look at fat Marion. I didn't like fleshiness. I have the spirit of an acolyte, pure and clean. I don't like sweating and sneezing and blowing your nose and those other horrible things that boys go on about all the time, and this other thing - I was not doing it. Just not. Never. A thing like that would not happen to me. I saw it happen to Marion, all the whisperings and pains that you couldn't say what they were, and it all kept hidden like a nameless contamination that must be kept out of the world's view. I didn't want to grow up. I would not become a woman if this awful smearing shameful juiciness, this dreadful spreading uncontainable stain is part of it. And it hadn't happened to me, even though I was older than Marion was when it happened to her. That's because I stopped eating when I began to grow. And it all stopped. I hovered below the crucial body weight (quote from the doctor).

I intended to stay just as I was - never have to wear tight clothes, or high heels, or lipstick, or put rollers in my hair, powder on my face, be nice to boys, make conversation. I wouldn't be looked at. That would be the worst, to know that everybody was looking at your bum or your bosom. I could go about being my usual invisible self, just left to do my own things and never be commented upon, like a fairy at the bottom of the garden. I liked being bone thin. I felt as if I could fly. There's just some little trick to it that I hadn't found out yet.

But of course they rowed. The tears, the yelling, the nagging, the pleading, the understanding talks, the persuasion, bribery and corruption: *Think of your mother, think of your father, think of your sister, think of your future, of course you like boys, of course you want to look your best, would you like a trip to the hairdresser, but you would be so pretty if only you'd eat, I made it specially for you...*

I liked my odd Irish granny. She leaves me alone. We used to come here for holidays when I was little. But that was long ago. Then mum got her job, and for some reason that stopped us going to Ireland, and we went to Marbella or the Algarve or Tuscany, or Orlando. I travelled to granny's on my own - first time, with a ticket round my neck, like a parcel.

The first thing granny did was take me into the garden. She spends all her time in the garden, even when it's raining. That's how I get so much time to myself. She showed me round the garden. It's like a jungle. I don't know what she does out there all the time. Everything's enormous and all mixed up through each other - in a mess really, but she has it a different way in her head. She explained how the garden lay diagonally to the points of the compass, so that each corner points straight north or south or whatever. She took me to the gateway with an arch over it.

She said, "And this is the north - and look..."

She lifted up some big floppy leaves at the foot of the archway and there were big stones underneath - smooth green stones with great big splashes of red on them, as if streaked with blood. "These are my guardian stones" she said, "When I first saw them I didn't like them, because of the red on them. But they do no harm here. They keep me safe from the north, like human sacrifice to ward off evil. And look over here..." and she scurried across the back of the house, to another corner, where there were paving stones and a view along the side of the house, over a fence, to the sea, very far off or so it seemed. "The wind howls through here in winter" she said "The west wind from the sea. This is my favourite corner. You can see the sunset from here, beautiful, and on a stormy day the air smells salty. This is where I have my angels." And she pointed at a layer of stones of all sizes that edged the paving. They were grey, rounded, with a single white line that marked out a circle on each stone.

"When your dad was small, he found one on the beach and said it was an angel because it had a halo. So of course, I just had to have some angels, and after that every time we went to the beach I brought back an angel, because I needed them to guard the west, as many as I could find, because the west can be tricky. The west can be very dangerous. It has the lure of other lands in it, of Tir-na-og. That's why the old hermits built their stone houses as far west as possible and sat there, praying their heads off. I like to think of this whole western corner of the garden shimmering with angels, all hovering and singing in the air, like a cloud of midges."

My mother had said to me, privately, getting me ready to come here, that Granny was as mad as a hatter, and she wasn't sure that this was the right place for me, and that if granny got too strange I must phone home at least once and be fetched. All this had made me feel a lot better about going. I decided, standing in granny's cloud of angels that I liked it here, and that I would never go home. Granny herself was a bit the way I imagined angels, somewhat shrunken and with a dry powdery skin, gone beyond the juiciness of my mother and Marion, less earthen than ordinary people, her very physical substance drained and somewhat faded, as if from the right angle, in the right light, she would be translucent, edging towards invisibility. This was how I thought of angels - purified out of earthly nature, invisible and able to fly. My flesh was shrinking, my bones thinning. Absence of food was lightening me.

Granny loved her food, eaten in strange combinations and at

strange hours. She told me to take what I wanted from the cupboard or from the garden, and if she was cooking she made extra for me and put it on a plate. But she never argued about me eating and would give my untouched food to the dogs without comment. I ate somethings some times, not often, and only things that allowed me to remain light, and grow lighter.

I sometimes helped granny in the garden. In fact I kept myself very much confined to the garden. On this particular day I was helping her pot on some foxglove seedlings, tiny little things.

"They'll not bloom until next year" she said, "They need time to get their feet properly under them, just like some people, and then you'd never credit how big they get."

I dabbled my fingers in compost, tucking in the tiny roots, "Where will you plant them?"

"They need the right place, to suit their nature. They like shade. I think they'll go beside the wall."

Lifting and sifting handfuls of earth, I found a fragment of seashell.

"Granny, is it far from here to the sea?"

"No. You can walk there."

"Do you ever go?"

"No. I never go now. Used to of course. You have to climb some rocks and fences. I'll show you."

"To go myself?"

"Why not? But take something to eat with you. You'll get hungry if you're away long." and she pulled some ripened pods from among the rows of peaplants and slipped them into the pocket of my cardigan.

Then she showed me the path to the sea. We went up the road slightly and stopped at a rusty gate. It was a high barred gate that had to be climbed, but that would be easy; and beyond was an untarred lane running westwards under stunted sycamores.

"It doesn't go all the way mind." Granny said. "It ends at another gate. Just climb it and follow your nose, and you'll be there. Mind you, there's no sand, just rocks."

My mother would have given me a catalogue of safety

instructions and then have decided she'd better come too, and have sulked about it because she really wanted to be doing something else.

Granny just waved cheerio and then scampered off back along the road to her garden harbour. Slightly scared, but excited and determined to reach the sea, I dropped off the top bar of the gate and set off along the greeny, shadowy, midgey lane. The air was full of these tiny, jigging insects that caught the filtered sunlight like dust motes, and bit continuously. I could see why granny hadn't come this way for years. I plucked a stem of bracken from the ditch, and waving it vigorously about my head to keep the midges off, traversed the lane, the other gate, and leaving the midges behind, two fields, empty of cattle, but littered abundantly with cow dung.

I climbed a slight rise and found myself looking down on a stony pebbly edging to a blue summery sea. I dropped to my knees to conceal my presence, very slowly, for further along, on the shingle, two fox cubs were playing like puppies, dancing about and around each other, playing tug of war with lengths of seaweed. This was the loneliest, most private far-away place that I'd ever been, and I'd found it all by myself. I sat and watched the foxes for about an hour, and began to eat the peas that granny had stored in my pocket.

I went there every day, all summer. Every day granny would give me something out of the garden, peas, radishes, tiny carrots, bits of lettuce, and later raspberries, gooseberries, currants of all colours. I took my sketchbook with me and drew. I'd never been happier. Granny didn't care if my clothes, flapping loosely on my bony shoulders were filthy. She never said anything about my hair or wanted me to wear lipstick, or high heel shoes or to try on jumpers in shops, just to see did the colour suit me. Even when she drove into town for messages granny let me be. She wasn't much better herself. The pair of us were a disgrace - granny all shrunken with age in her Oxfam finery with a hat on, and me all shrunken by something else in my flapping, raggedy jeans.

It was good to be let be, and the weather was kind that summer. I was able to go out and about every day, my pockets full of fruit or sometimes a piece of scone bread lifted from the kitchen table. I explored as much of the rocky coast as I was able to climb over. There were cliffs I had no intention of trying. I didn't want to be an angel yet. My greatest pleasure though was to find a good rock close to the surge of the waves and sit there, idly watching the rise and fall of the foam, the dripping of the wet rocks, the pouring of the water, the colours of the waves. And I began to think more and more of mermaids - most often when I perched somewhere to watch the sun set. I would wedge myself just out of the reach of the water. At that hour, often, the wind would drop, and the swell and lift of the waves among the rocks would grow lazy, gentle and rounded as breathing in and out. The rocks and land would grow ponderous and the sea and sky, greedy, would suck up all the light. The sea would run in among the rocks dappled with a mix of sunset light and dark green shadows from the land, and where these shapes and lights juggled and slid one over the other in the meeting of water and land, and where sometimes a lazy arm of seaweed stirred from below to elbow the surface and sink, there I became more and more sure, I would one day see mermaids, there were the sea met the land, by the mazing light of the setting sun, when the sea breathed against the rocks as gently as a sleeping child.

I filled my sketchbooks in anticipation with mermaids - drifting, drowning, floating mermaids. I gave them seaweedy hair and drew currents of water around them and fitted their bodies into this flow. I lavished detail on their tails and hair and gave them all rounded shoulders and breasts and swelling stomachs above their fishy tails, because that was the way I knew they were, full-fleshed, and never weighty because they swam in the water as if they were flying. Anything too slender would be washed away, melted; mermaids had to be rounded to exist. They were like the rounded beach stones, smooth and firm, no corners; mermaids for all they swam and were fishy were as solid as the earth. I gathered shells and felt their swelling roundness, I liked to find round stones that fitted my palm and carry them with me, all day. As I wandered I rolled granny's round, pearly green peas on my tongue, palmed small hard half ripe apples that had begun to drop from her trees, bit into their bitter flesh.

Some days I would not go to the shore, I'd be so busy with my mermaids. I'd find some green cave in the garden, and stay there all day, bringing in handfuls of garden fruits to eat as I drew. The raspberries were quickly over. They stained my pockets red. Granny was mean about the strawberries. She wanted them kept to be eaten at suppertime. I gave in on this. She made such a ceremony of it.

The two of us sat with basins of water, washing and hulling the floating strawberries and then shared the arduous task of whipping cream with a fork. And then she would set castor sugar in a silver topped shaker, and her best Waterford dishes on a tray with a linen cloth. She liked best to eat the strawberries at sunset, at the rickety folding table at the western corner of the house as the last light left the sky.

"It's as if somebody had pulled the plug," she said, "and all the light just poured down the plughole."

"It's not like that," I said, "There's another land under the water, where the sun goes at night, and there's no earth, no rock, no bones, everything is soft and floats."

Sometimes we sat in the dark and waited for the moon; sometimes the evening grew so quiet that I was sure I could hear the sea, even at this distance. Granny once said she thought she could hear the dew falling. I said that I thought I could hear the snails sliding through the grass. She said that she was going to get her torch and her brick to murder them before they got her flowers.

I'll never forget that summer. I began to put on weight. I didn't mind. I really didn't. I felt a softness grow on me. I became my own body and allowed myself to flow freely into every corner of myself. When I breathed in I breathed right to the very soles of my feet. And when, one evening, alone by granny's angels, just as the sun set, I felt unfold between my legs the warm blood of womanhood, I did not feel contaminated or ashamed. I felt that I flowed like the tides of the sea, splendidly. I stopped drawing mermaids a short while after that.

Man and Wife

by Philip McClean

*A*t the tender age of six it was quite clear to me that life was all about boys and girls. Simple as that. Having come to terms with this I was to be confronted by a series of events which were to affect my understanding of this fact of life for many years to come.

Julie was her name. She was blonde and polite. She sat next to me in class on some occasions and, indeed, it might be said that we were the best of friends to start with.

She was a girl of distinction. She was saintly. She always shared her break time snack with me. She was wholly devoted to my welfare in a healthy platonic sense. She even helped me put my 'plus' and 'minus' signs in the right place, as Maths was never my strong point. However, reading was and in time I saw it as my duty, as well as a great pleasure, to sit beside Julie on the floor during reading time. This of course was in order to correct some of her occasional grammatical errors. Soon I began to realise that I had ulterior motives in performing these "acts of mercy."

There were early indications that I was indeed beginning to lose control of the situation. The real world began to be invaded by misty fantasies which were stimulated by our teacher, Mrs Donnelley and her insatiable appetite for the more surreal work of C.S. Lewis and Tolkein. While the class sat in transfixed awe at her feet during "The Lion, The Witch and the Wardrobe" I was plagued by urges to escort Julie to the nearest cupboard, the one next to the nature table, and walk hand in hand into Narnia. I would turn to her and smile and she would look right into my eyes knowingly. She knew what I was thinking - What a woman.

It was after two days of this sort of pressure that I finally decided to make my move. I was a decisive child. I knew then what I wanted and waited only till break time to expose my thoughts to my beloved.

"Julie" I said tenderly, "Will you marry me?"

She looked up from the chocolate bar she was munching. It was then I realised the maturity of the girl. She was never one to be blown by the winds of foolish impulse.

"Maybe" she replied smiling. This was of course more than I hoped for and more than any decent lad could expect. Besides women of real class were never rushed into casual relationships. I was overjoyed and knew that women in general meant yes when they said "maybe." I had learned that from my mother.

I was right and it was obviously an event that must be carried off with all due haste. Six year old girls are not known for their discretion and so the marriage was on everybody's lips by the time lunch-time came.

Jimmy Hegarty, a rather snivelling "youngster" suggested that I should first ask my mother. I told him that courtesy required the bridegroom to ask the father of the bride and I would do that after school. Elizabeth Jane McCauley said that it was only "puppy love". She later told Mrs Donnelley that I had slapped her on the face with my ruler - which I had! My love was definitely not to be compared with a common animal!

The short walk from the school to her home was a triumphant march, hand in hand with my dearest I set my face towards my goal. I anticipated no real difficulty in persuading her father, besides wasn't it every father's dream to match his daughter off with a fine lad? Indeed I thought that he should be really pleased to have Julie off his hands. I had a future to offer her.

I was going to be the head of the Army and the Navy. It was only a matter of time. Certainly no adult who ever asked ever gave me any cause to think that this was not my vocation in life.

"What do you want to do when you grow up?" they would ask.

"The Head of the Army and the Navy"

"Very good. You'll have to work hard at school Michael and you just never know!"

Being a trusting child I thought that my career prospects were excellent. I just had a little growing up to do. Julie's father was a peculiar sort. He seemed to be at home a lot. He watched more television than my mother said was good for me. When I arrived he was still watching television with a newspaper on his lap with his feet on a stool. He grunted "Hello" in a rather hasty manner. I felt tense. Despite my bold spirit I felt an icebreaker was necessary.

"It'll give you square eyes" I quipped. He didn't even notice or acknowledge my intrusion. I could see that the man was beyond reasoning. "Excuse me Mr Greenmore" I said, "Julie and I want to get married and so..."

He guffawed so loudly and so ungraciously that he spat the cup of tea he was drinking all over the television set. This was a major setback. Here was I trying to make a decent girl of his daughter and all the insufferable man could do was laugh. However, my doubts soon changed to elation as he replied, "Why sure my man. Yes sure why not?" He guffawed again but this time he did not spill his tea and so, pleased at both his response and obvious joy at finding a new son-in-law, my love and I skipped happily out of the room.

"Well then" I said in a very assertive way, 'we must set a date".

"How about tomorrow at lunchtime?" She said.

"Fine with me darling." I had a smile on my face from ear to ear and just as I was thinking I was the happiest man alive, it happened! She gave the most sloppy succulent kiss on my cheek.

"No. No" I cried trying to restrain her at arms length to prevent her from doing this again.

"What are you doing?" I cried, "it's not right" My thoughts were on the time my mother had told me that if she ever caught me kissing "the wee girls" she would sell me to the gypsies! What is this woman doing I thought. As the leader of the relationship I felt it my duty, and an urgent one at that, to tell her what was wrong.

"It's not right you know!" She laughed and said that it was only a 'wee kiss'. Besides we were betrothed.

"Only a kiss" I said adopting a really knowing tone, "you're only allowed to kiss after we're married and then only once or twice."

Fortunately she saw her wrong and said she supposed that I was right. I felt however, that there was some need for active reconciliation. I spent all my 5p pocket money on a 'lucky dip'. She got a plastic model of the Eiffel Tower and I got the sweets inside.

However I gave the candy to her on principle. She then said that she loved me more than Jimmy Hegarty. Aha! What's this I thought, so that explains his sour-faced attitude.

When I quizzed her about it she then refuted loving him at all. But the damage was done. A man in such a state of infatuation was susceptible to feelings of envy which, no matter how oversized, remained as an ominous black cloud on the horizon of bliss.

The next day was bright and chilly as I remember. The union had been set for lunchtime. We did not have a minister but the next best thing to one; a minister's son. Aaron Wetherall was the son of a distinguished Church of Ireland minister. It was only fitting that he exercise his birthright and marry us. I had the greatest respect for his father. Indeed it was he who had thrilled most of the lads when he came along to school assembly and told us about his war experiences. That was a highly popular talk and much more interesting than Mr McCleary our Headmaster telling us that the difference between bad children and good children was obedience. We all knew that was the case.

The sun shone brightly that lunchtime and, it being late autumn, a carpet of brown and crinkled leaves littered the playground. I sat on the railings with Jamie Daly and "Kiddo" Bryson. I paced through the leaves and rolled them underfoot trying to think straight. Jamie was persuading Bryson to give him some of his chewing gum but Bryson said it was his last piece.

"This relationship" I suddenly thought "Is going to end in disaster." There was no denying it. The real problem was one of accommodation.

There was just no more room in our house and besides it was going to mean sacrifices like not getting as many biscuits from the evening's supper dividend.

I already had three brothers, one sister and a cat, not forgetting mother and father. Besides all these practical difficulties I had doubts about the fidelity of the girl. Anyone who could seriously consider Jimmy Hegarty as a partner had problems of guide-dog proportions.

I rose from the railing to my full height. I was oblivious to the brawl in the leaves which was now raging over the chewing gum issue. As I entered the school building I could just make out a muffled scream as Jamie Daly forced a fistful of wet rotten leaves into Kiddo's mouth.

She was sat on the benches outside Room 11 with two skinny twins and Master Hegarty. By now the reader must appreciate my lack of respect for small talk.

"Julie", I spluttered, "It's off." She maintained her calm and smiling sweetly retorted,

"That's all right Michael I had forgotten anyway."

The bell sounded and class resumed as normal. Jimmy Hergarty was kept in by Mrs Donnelley for fifteen minutes after school on a charge of pestering Elizabeth Jane McCauley. He always did lack class.

K Twice

by Irene Maxwell

My first thought was, "Show off bloody Englishman" as he stood surrounded by laughing faces in the enormous stone-flagged French hostel kitchen - in what had once been a castle.

Seconds later I stood stock still; paralysed; overcome by an attraction so blow swift that all these years later I recall it and grieve a little.

He was golden bronze colour - even his hair, and this was like the tight innocent curls on a Boticelli cherub, making the marvellously shrewd puck face blaze in wild contrast.

He stood there, feet apart, hands on hips, holding forth in a twangy Cockney accent on the only way to cook squid; and the French and Italian men and girls around him in a circle were weak with laughter aiding and abetting him, shouting in· French - gesturing, as he pranced around the kitchen where the more staid Germans and English stood grinning.

Suddenly he said Cockney sharp, "What's up Irish - not amused?" - and I realised that I must have been staring so intensely, totally fascinated by him, that my face had taken on what my mother called its "turf spade" look - long and lugubrious.

"Oh God" I thought, "He's talking to me - dear God they're all looking at me now" and I blushed overall and turned away clumsily, blindly.

He shouted, "C'mon Irish, help me with the spaghetti". My arm was grabbed and I was hauled awkward and graceless into the middle of the group around that grubby cooker.

He bombarded me with wisecracks all the time that he was dealing with the food, prodding the revolting mess in one great black saucepan; swirling around the spaghetti in another and yelling instructions about dishes, forks, bread, wine to the others.

In twenty minutes the meal was ready and I was plonked down beside him at the huge wooden table. It was all a great babble of talk and laughter and I sat dazed, poking tentatively at this weird concoction, drinking in the Englishman's every word.

Right behind his head, framing the bronze curls was a white alcove and I remember the amber coloured jar with three huge blood red gladioli in it.

The talk scrabbled over and around me; half of it incomprehensible, my French was so schoolgirlish. Every now and then the little Cockney would turn right round to me and I'd get scraps and bits of information about him. He was twenty, three years older than me - an apprentice solicitor - now on his usual two months stint of bumming around France. All this I took in as he held court at that table.

Then as abruptly as ever he looked me full in the face - very dark blue eyes steady and enquiring,

"Well Irish, what about you then?"

and I stammered,

"How did you know I was Irish?"; feeling awkward, white skinned, gauche, bog Irish, first time abroad, first time anywhere, wishing I was anywhere now at peace - at home - away from these bright, clever at-ease-in-their-bodies travellers.

He very gently put his hand against my cheek - but without changing the sharp wicked tone, "Saw you yesterday - made enquiries." Then he said very quietly, "I'll see you later - about ten at the gates - I'll show you the island."

Then he turned away as abruptly as ever and I might as well have not been there after that and all I could think was, "Is he making a fool of me? - will I stand there at the gate like a lost soul, getting amused stares from all the comers and goers?"

But I did meet him in the lovely warm night at the old fortress gate. He came striding out across the courtyard; the short stocky golden figure - still in shorts and sandals, and I nearly died of embarrassment in my flaring cotton dress. But all he said was, looking at this tall, dark, awkward girl, "Nice, Irish - c'mon love" and he unselfconsciously took my hand.

We wound our way down through the twisty little paths; through the pinewoods that surrounded the fortress. Every now and then I'd stop, listening to the cicadas.

"They're like crickets in the back of a turf fire", I said - and he would bend over laughing soundlessly. Then I'd glance sideways at him and join in the laugh because I could feel myself unclenching inside; all the tension going, just to be happy with him. We were descending all the time through shrubby, aromatic undergrowth right down to the dusky beach looking across at the lights glittering round Cannes.

I had never met anyone like him before - he was so quicksilver, so sure, and he drew from me all about my country background, the simplicity of it contrasting with his own city - knowingness. He would stop every now and again, looking at me very intently. I felt that feathery, blurry, lovely feeling that you get when you are gently and pleasantly tipsy. I told him funny stories about my mad uncle Jesse who had never recovered from the war and my equally mad religious-fanatic aunt Mary.

Suddenly he stopped again and said, "You're lovely Irish" and kissed my mouth and then we walked on very quietly down to the beach and lay there on the sand just looking out on to the velvety lapping water round the little boats at the jetty. Then he said, "C'mere" and held me very gently, just as you would an almost asleep baby and after a long time leaned his chin on my head and said, "You a Catholic Irish?"

"No," I said, "Why?"

"Nothing."

I twisted round and looked up at him! "What's your name?" - "Karl Kaye" - smiling.

"K Twice" I said.

Then the smile faded abruptly and he quickly put his hand across my mouth. "Don't tell me your name, Irish - I'm moving on tomorrow and I don't want to know it."

I think I knew at that moment what it must be like to be electrocuted, or run through with a rapier or anything that is cruelly swift and deadly. All I could do was to sit there - strangulated, numb, dumb, tightfaced.

"Have you to leave tomorrow?" I stuttered - "Honestly?"

"Oh Irish!...honestly or dishonestly, I have to go" and he held me close and rocked me backwards and forwards.

When we got back to the great gate in the wall it was firmly closed.

"We're locked out" he said.

Neither of us had a watch - we had forgotten all about time -

"The gate won't open 'till 5.30am or so" he said.

We quietly turned round and went back to the pinewoods and lay there very close and whispered and dozed.

"Bloody babes in the wood" he murmured sleepily once and I just lay and looked at him and thought how beautiful he was; how right in his body; in himself.

I felt a great surprising rage that he should have stepped into my life for only a minute and made me turn metal cartwheels for nothing. Then I laid my face down on his arm and he wakened and opening his arms wide and closed me right inside them as close as I ever could get to his body.

We walked back slowly through the brilliant mistiness of that French day-break. There were thousands of fine wispy spider webs across every bush; floating in the air, trailing across our faces.

We scattered drops of dew from every twig and didn't feel the chill of it on our bodies.

I stopped suddenly and flicked pearling moisture from his forehead.

"Dew boy" I laughed. He stiffened suddenly; his face mask-like. Then at my questioning glance he suddenly relaxed and grinned, "Bog Irish - that's what you are - Bog Irish."

I wondered when the sadness - panic would set in - but we wandered on and quite suddenly it was full day; not slowly and tentatively like an Irish morning; slow fingers of light slivering out again from the darkness, but sudden brightness with the whole island drying and starting its noise again.

The hostel was open. He said, "I'm leaving very soon. Get a few hour's sleep but go out on to the parapet outside your dormitory when you go in and I'll wave to you" - gay, lighthearted - throwaway.

I felt stupid; inarticulate. I wanted to have the knowledge, the guile, the experience to tell him how much I wished to know him better and better for a long, long time. Surely we could write - something. All I said was,

"All right."

We leaned from our separate parapets outside the still dormitories. I looked and looked at him, all golden in the morning sun.

We looked across at each other for a long, long time and strangely, slowly I felt a great peacefulness wiping out all the panic - hurt. It was such a strong feeling; as if we were touching physically.

"Goodbye Irish" - and it was a kiss; a caress.

Someone handed me a note later in the day; one of the Frenchmen who had shared that memorable meal. On the front was printed "IRISH."

"Is it you?" he smiled.

I nodded. The writing inside was unexpectedly neat. It said,

"I'm marrying a nice Jewish girl I've known all my life in six months time. I can't ever know your name or anything more." K. Twice.

The Tooth Witch

by Simon Kerr

She sat in the silent, bleached-out hospital waiting room. Praying for someone behind the doors that carried the ominous headline OPERATING THEATRES to give her some news. But it was a long wait before news came. A long time to think, and fidget, and regret. She'd always told Joe not to fidget, smacked him for it even, but he was highly strung, and still did it...bad boy...poor bad Joe. For goodness sake, why wasn't she being told what was wrong with him?

The doors finally clattered open. Shrouded in green and white paper garments spotted with brown blood, a surgeon rustled his way into the waiting room. As he pulled his mask down and let his eyes fall on her, she caught the copper-salt odour of his trade and turned her pinched nose up even more than usual.

"Mrs Audrey Aspin?"

"Yes doctor?" she replied. He was looking at her as intently as a dentist bent on an extraction. His old-as-time face pale, and strained. Was he looking at her mouth? No, she was just being her old paranoid self.

"We're just operating on your son Joseph. We've managed to patch up the considerable damage to his esophagus and stomach. There may be damage lower down because as yet we haven't located whatever caused the tearing. Can you tell me, did Joseph eat anything out of the ordinary - something sharp - before you rushed him in earlier today?"

"No, no," she shrugged, "not that I know of doctor. But then, I don't oversee all his eating anymore. He might have disobeyed me and eaten some sweets or chocolates. I keep telling him, "You'll choke on those" but he doesn't listen to me. No, he thinks he knows it all. At his age. What do you know when you're eight, eh doctor? Nothing but what you're told, that's what."

"Yes, yes," said the doctor without conviction. It was obvious he did not share her stricture. "Well," he continued, "we'd better take Joseph down to X-ray again, see if we can't find what's in his lower digestive tract. We'll keep you informed. Okay?"

She nodded, and watched as he rustled back to play his part in the drama of the theatres within.

"Sweeties!" Audrey cursed. Naughty boy. Boiled sweets could cut the roof of a child's mouth to shreds in a few sugary sucks. Yes. That's what he'd done. Even when he knew what had happened to her teeth.

She had to wear dentures now and forever because she'd never been told to clean her teeth as a child. Nobody had cared. Indeed, the Tooth Fairy had rewarded her for every spot of decay, every tooth lost. By the age of eighteen, she'd lost all her incisors, premolars, canines, and eventually, had to have the last of her molars removed. She got plenty of money for them though. Enough to feed her craving for more sweets. More sweets which made her fat. Ugly. Unloved. Untouched by boys throughout the desires of her teens; untouched, even by herself.

So lonely.

And her mother didn't do the right thing. Didn't stop the Tooth Fairy, who was the Tooth Fairy, for goodness sake! She just kept on treating 'mummy's little girly' to the things her own mother had denied her in the name of economy as a child.

It was on her eighteenth birthday as she stood in front of the cruel wardrobe mirror that she saw herself for what she really was: a weak, spoiled brat. In that moment, years too late, Audrey decided to break the mould of her mouth: of her life.

She packed her meagre possessions and left her mother to dote and damage the shadow of a father to death. She travelled from her native Kent up to London. Found a job as a secretary in Lloyds, the financial heart of the City. Time went by. Time well spent. She went on a crash diet. Lost three stones in two months, getting herself down to the Cosmo-says weight for her five foot three frame. When she could afford it, she bought herself an American Dream pair of dentures; so good that it was almost impossible to see that her teeth were totally artificial.

She went through the slow process of trying to like herself and almost got to. Self confidence and independence were within her reach when others seemed to start liking the new her too.

A middle-aged stockbroker by the name of Geoffrey Haimes began to stop by her desk at lunchtimes. He wasn't the Cary Grant she dreamed of being swept away by; even a bit of a fop from at first glance, but he seemed to be a sincere man.

He asked her out.

Bathing in her new found confidence she agreed to see him.

Of course, she had to be wary what to eat on their dinner dates, in case her dentures fell out. And what to say, in case her dentures fell out. And how to kiss - no tongues - in case her dentures fell out and mortified her.

Her lack of teeth was never far from her thoughts, spoiling, foiling, spoiling.

He asked her to marry him on bended knee after two months of tempered courtship. The gold ring he proffered shone more brightly than his bald head and was studded with more best friends than she'd ever had, or was ever going to have; still, her answer was a shaky: "I'll think about it."

There was little joy in the moment, her heart did not flutter far before dread clipped its wings: what would he think of her teeth in a glass beside their honeymoon bed?

Despite her reservations, Geoffrey pressed his suit continuously and confronted her one evening on the threshold of her flat. His beady eyes were full of want. "I love you," he stated quietly, "and I know you love me more than a little. Why are you holding back?"

"I can't tell you."

"I want you to be able to tell me everything."

"Everything?"

"Yes," he replied, sincerely. So sincerely.

She wanted to tell him, but how could she? "I have no teeth," she cried out before she knew what she was saying.

"What?"

"Look." She took out her dentures - covered in chewed up dinner - and showed them to him, expecting him to run a mile.

Instead he said, "It doesn't matter. I love you."

He truly loved her. She remembered being taken aback at the liberation she felt. What did her lack of teeth matter?

It didn't.

At least, not for a while.

They got married. She moved in with him; gave up her job; became the proper little housewife he wanted. Things were...fine. Happy even. He made love to her, bare gums and all, as passionately as he could. But then, one cold December morning, after a year or so, she caught him staring at the glass on the bedside table...at her soaking dentures with what could only have been...disgust on his face. From then on, he'd closed his eyes when they made love - all the time. Eventually, he only closed his eyes to go to sleep.

Her Geoffrey had lied. It did matter.

She cried and ground her gums when she thought of his rejection. There was no doubt he was slipping away and the feeling of loss was more painful than all the extraction she'd had to endure put together because she knew that this would leave her empty: void of teeth, void of soul.

She needed something to cling to. They'd talked about having children but Geoffrey wasn't keen. A baby, yes. It seemed like the way to keep him and the lifestyle she had become accustomed to.

Conception, her salvation, was surprisingly simple: she got Geoffrey so drunk he didn't even notice the theft of his sperm. The pregnancy was trying, but after nine months of strange cravings for unchewable foods and a heaving period of morning sickness, she gave birth to Joseph Henry Haimes. She swore on the pain of her final contraction that delivered 'Joe' to the wailing world that even if she was not the best wife in the world, she would be the best mother there ever was.

And, even through a dull divorce in which she won the full custodial rights to Joe; the run of their martial mansion, and half her husband's fortune, she had never failed to keep that promise. The years of careful tuition...

Her thoughts were suddenly obscured by the hurried re-entry of the rustling doctor. He looked agitated. She heard him say, "Mrs Aspin.."

"What is it? What's wrong?" She refused to move until she had some answers.

"I'm afraid to tell you that although we've completed the procedure, Joseph's condition has become critical. We're moving him to Intensive Care."

"Oh my goodness. How?"

"The latest X-ray charts show the problem was much more complicated than we originally diagnosed. Joseph's small intestine was badly damaged by what he swallowed. He was bleeding internally. We managed to stop that but throughout the surgery he was calling out."

"For me?"

"No, Mrs Aspin. Who or what is the 'Tooth Witch'?"

"Eh.." she said, her gaze bound to the floor.

The Tooth Witch and the spoken words of her spell lashed Audrey as the doctor stared on -

"If you don't clean your teeth the Tooth Witch will slap you.

If you don't floss your teeth the Tooth Witch will smack you.

If you have to get a filling the Tooth Witch will hit you.

If your teeth come out of your mouth - in any which way - the Tooth Witch will beat you to within an inch of your life."

The magic of his guardian was unusual, and painful sometimes, but it worked. Joe never had a filling. Upon every check-up his dentist proclaimed Joe's mouth the healthiest in his practice. Audrey was really proud of that. He had not and would not be teased by his school friends - of which he had many - because he binged on sweets and ignored the laws of dental hygiene.

She looked after him; perhaps less now than in his infant past but she was still vigilant. A case in point was his birthday last month. Joe was playing with his new toys in her living room with all the friends she'd invited. The time came to light the candles on the cake. All eight. Joe blew them all out in one big puff. Everybody cheered. Sang 'Happy Birthday To You' and ate a slice of cake. Joe had pleaded for some too. She refused him with a scowl. While she wasn't looking he must have taken a piece of cake. She caught him later on, hiding under the table, gobbling it. She seized the plate; cast it down; took him by the arm and marched him straight to the bathroom to clean his teeth. Then she sent him to his room and told all his friends that he was ill and that the party was over.

She acted this way because she loved Joe. She'd done other things like that too, all for him.

He'd entered his school's annual fancy dress competition when he was six, dressed as Al Capone. Gangster hat, suit, and big fake cigar. She helped him make the costume. He came third overall. He was so pleased; his little elfin face so red with pleasure. She'd cheered and cheered. Until she found out what his prize was. Of course she took the chocolate bar off Joe, and wrote a strongly worded letter of complaint to the headmistress. The headmistress wrote back: she couldn't see the harm in giving a child one chocolate bar. The cheek of it! Audrey removed Joe from that school to a more disciplined environment.

Sometimes, with children, you had to be cruel to be kind. Not all the time, though. She wasn't a monster.

"Mrs Aspin..." She looked up with a start. There was the doctor again, talking, "...your son seems terrified by the name. Even under the anaesthetic."

"Name?" She struggled to pick up the conversation but then managed to catch a thread. "Oh, yes. What was he saying?"

The doctor frowned deeply. "Strangely coherent sentences which are unusual when a patient is unconscious, like 'I didn't mean to' and 'Don't let her take me'."

"I don't know where all this is leading us. What exactly is wrong with my son, doctor?"

"Your son swallowed one of his teeth. That in itself is a strange occurrence. However, his case is somewhat stranger. This tooth, it is by all accounts a very unusual looking molar, the roots of which - and I know how far-fetched this must sound - were so sharp that they have cut through the lining of most of his upper digestive tract."

"That's impossible," she gasped, "I've made sure Joseph has all his adult teeth."

"I personally removed it no less than twenty-five minutes ago or I wouldn't have believed it myself," the doctor insisted.

"How could a perfectly healthy tooth just fall out?" Audrey asked incredulously.

Perfectly healthy teeth don't just fall out," replied the doctor.

"Well then.."

"Mrs Aspin, your son's tooth is really rotten. Look at it." He removed the tooth from a pocket in his gown and held it up under one of the sterile hospital lights. Two unnaturally sharp roots shone menacingly. She shuddered to think what they'd done to her poor son's stomach. But decay? Yes. Sure enough, Audrey, an expert on tooth decay if anyone was, could see decay.

She remembered Joe trying to say something to her last week. She'd been watching the News at Ten; she hadn't been paying attention. He spat something onto the floor while speaking. She waved him away: didn't see what it was. It must have been the tooth. Was he trying to confess to her about it then?

"How is that possible?" She stabbed her index finger at a huge black hole of decay. How could Joe have let this happen? How could she have let this happen? The answer was simple. Entrusting him to his own fear, she hadn't inspected his mouth for a month. Her slackness was a crime that might just as easily have been perpetrated by her own mother.

"Judging by the minor infection I observed in his gums, I would say he'd been keeping the rotten thing in his mouth for weeks," answered the doctor.

"What?" gasped Audrey.

"I'm no psychiatrist, but I would hazard a guess it has something to do with this damned Tooth Witch character. Like I said, he kept saying that name. He was terrified of her."

A nurse came clattering through the doors to the theatres. Her head was shaking. "Doctor. Mrs Aspin. I'm sorry to have to tell you this. Joseph. His heart stopped beating. We've tried to revive him but he'd lost too much blood and didn't respond."

Audrey stared in horror as the doctor sighed, failure seemingly adding another hundred years to his face. "Not my Joe?" she wailed.

Tears sprouted down her cheeks and into her mouth; the salt bitter on the false teeth of the best mother there ever was.

Catharsis

by Michael Smyth

The Brian Moore Short Story Awards" - the announcement caught his eye and his imagination. Wasn't it said that everybody had at least one good novel in them? That might be a little ambitious, but a short story should be possible.

"2000 words." He recalled the essays and assignments he'd written in the past. A4 paper. 320 words to the page. Six and a quarter pages. One page for the introduction. One and a half pages for the ending. Three and three quarter pages for the body of the story. "Easy!" he decided, excited by the thought.

All he needed was the subject matter. The Troubles? No, no, not the Troubles. Everybody will write about the bloody Troubles! A new angle? There wasn't one, he concluded in exasperation. Young love thwarted by religion?, families torn apart by the conflict?, political intrigue? - they'd all been done to death in print, on television or the cinema. He was convinced that the Troubles would only end when the BBC and Hollywood had wrung the last storyline out of the situation.

Science fiction? Knew nothing about it.

Romance? Mindless drivel for the feckless in the population.

He began to realise that this might not be so straightforward. Yet he remained confident that he could deliver the goods once he got the right topic. That was the key!

An old joke crossed his mind. The class had to write an essay and the teacher told them that their stories would be more interesting if they were built around religion, the family and sex, with a mystery element added for good measure. A week later the pupils turned up with pages of complex plots. Apart from little Johnny, who produced just one line - "Oh God, my sister's pregnant and she doesn't know who the father is!"

He always smiled when he recalled that joke, not just because the punch line was good, but also for the way Johnny had played by the rules and still beat the system.

He realised it was only a gag, but wondered if there might not be something to it. Maybe if his story included at least some of the elements the 'teacher' had suggested, it could be a winner.

"They met at University, when he was in the third year and she had just started. A year older than him, she'd spent time on Voluntary Service, and then travelled the hippy trail through Afganistan and India. Losing interest in the wandering, she sought something with greater purpose.

A law degree - something to work for, something which would get her places, something with big earnings potential. The gypsy life was fine for a while, but success, comfort and luxury were three stations further down the track, and she aimed to be on the train going there.

He was hooked from the moment they met, seeing in her the energy and drive he lacked. For her, he represented the standards her father had stood for, although she never fully appreciated them when he was alive. He was controlled, hard working and dependable and in a volatile world full of crazy people, these were things she was increasingly coming to value.

Her mother was alive, but had been lost to dementia years ago. Her sister in Canada was engulfed in developing her medical practice. As an only child with both parents dead he had inherited the small terraced house he was born in. There were no family misgivings to have to contend with when they decided, less than three months after meeting, to marry. Even before the wedding she moved in and began making a home for their first daughter, Charlotte, who arrived within the year.

She'd planned the birth for the month after first year exams, and Rachel arrived at almost the same time the following year. He qualified and was earning his first teacher's salary by the time the second child was born. The routine which first attracted her to him now allowed her time to concentrate on her studies. It was no surprise when she topped the class and was invited to join McCartney, Pollock & Associates.

He couldn't have been happier. Comfortable as Head of

Department, he had a job with responsibility he could handle and authority which allowed him to integrate his domestic and school duties. He would rise early in the mornings to prepare breakfast for the family before dropping the kids off at the childminders on his way to work. In the afternoons he organised a timetable to allow him to pick up the children and have the evening meal on the table by 6 o'clock, when she returned home from work. The household was built on routine, and he was never more content than when everything went to plan. As it did for those first few months.

Then the odd 'office meeting' and the occasional 'training session' began to delay her return home. 'Extra responsibilities' started to keep her late on a regular basis. He knew she was ambitious and she argued well that these were opportunities that rarely arose and couldn't be turned down. He never disputed the logic, but inside grew more and more frustrated and angry at the disruption to their lives.

As the late nights increased and her 'work' overflowed into the weekends, he seethed inside and suspicions formed. And then he knew she was having an affair - all the signs were there - evidence stared him in the face. The phone calls from 'work' which she always took in the kitchen. The late nights. And accusing him of being obsessed with "bloody routines". Oh yes, he'd read about the guilty ones who tried to find faults in their partners in order to excuse their treachery.

What a fool he'd been! He'd given her a home, supported her financially though University and at the start of her professional life, virtually brought up the children on his own and now ran the house while she carried on with some high flyer from work.

Incessantly these thoughts battered his mind. As the certainty grew that he was right, so did his bitterness over how she had used him.

What to do? Challenge her? - she'd deny it and she and her lover would laugh at his predicament later. Stop her staying out late? - how? He could beat her, but she was a lawyer and would have him in court, probably in front of her favourite judge. He'd be slandered, convicted, written about in the papers and sacked - disaster!

With divorce he would lose half of his family home. She brought nothing to the marriage but his home would have to be split with her. She would claim custody of the children, and a considerable slice of his salary. And then, a couple of months later, she and her lover would become an 'item', and the children would have a new daddy - no way, no bloody way!

But how to get rid of the bitch, how to remove the poison which was destroying everything?

She was too smart, too cheating, too ruthless to negotiate with. She would have to be removed completely before anyone suspected that he knew what was going on. If she died soon no one would imagine him being involved. There were no skeletons in their martial cupboard - there was no motive.

How to kill her? Not with poison or over a cliff. Her death would have a sound explanation, and he would have an 'alibi' if it was ever required. And she would die - not injured, not in a coma - dead!

It took surprisingly little time to finalise his plan, but when complete and challenged from every angle, he knew it would work. The opportunity arrived soon afterwards, when she announced that she wouldn't be able to "get away from the office until about 8 o'clock tonight."

The kids were fast asleep at 7.30pm when he left, a little valium in their milk ensuring that they were unlikely to stir. The house remained lit during his absence and a tape machine in the hall would record any phone calls or knocks at the door. From this he would be able to calculate the time of any interruption. That would become the time he was having a bath, if anyone asked.

The crudely levelled site where she parked was about twenty minutes away, by bicycle. There were only four cars there when he arrived and her wondered which one belonged to her lover. He estimated, correctly as it turned out, that they would be too clever to be seen together.

In the near darkness she didn't see him lying across the front seats. He heard her footsteps falter as she tried to make out what it was that lay under the front of her car. As she leaned down to remove the rubble he'd placed there, he sat up and in the one motion turned his spare key to fire the engine to life. Already in gear, with the handbrake off, the car went over her before she even registered fear.

He stopped and took his key from the ignition. The absence of a pulse confirmed the obvious. Having located her keys, he took a six inch nail from his track suit top and jammed it under a front wheel. Restarting the engine with her key, he eased the vehicle forward. The tyre deflated in seconds. He jumped out, ran to his bicycle and was home before the police arrived at the car park. The whole exercise had taken less than 6- minutes. Within an hour he had washed, changed clothes and confirmed, through the tape, that there had been no phone calls or visitors. He was quietly sipping coffee and marking homeworks when the police knocked on the door.

The funeral was well attended. Word had spread that she struggled bravely to prevent the theft of her car, but had been run over as the thief panicked. The vehicle was abandoned after the puncture, with the driver getting away unseen. No clues were discovered at the scene and forensic examination confirmed that the culprit wore gloves.

While friends and colleagues offered transient sympathy and support, police interest evaporated once it was clear that there were no leads to follow.

The kids missed mummy, of course, but the relentless routine of their little lives somehow minimised the effect of her absence. At school he was seen as a stalwart doing a 'marvellous' job of raising the girls on his own. Compensation for her death afforded him the financial security he had always sought. Life settled into the predictable order he liked.

He would never again drop his guard or allow himself to be used. He had the girls, his pride and joy, and all things considered he reckoned that the outcome was not at all bad. He'd been hurt, but was now the stronger for it. He'd had to take risks but, overall, things had turned out quite satisfactorily."

Sensing the early rays of light filter through the study curtains, the writer checked his watch and discovered it was close to morning. He'd never written a story before and hadn't anticipated that the urge to commit himself to print would be quite so strong. His style might be too narrative but perhaps, with a bit of re-writing, the tale could become an interesting read. It had turned out to be quite exciting, but if it lacked credibility, he was unlikely to win any prize. However, if people did believe in the account, might some of them begin to remember and put two and two together? Would the police consider re-opening a long since closed file? Should he send in his entry?

Upstairs Charlotte and Rachael were still asleep when he decided that he would indeed enter the competition. After all, how much interest would the police take in a ten year old murder. And after more than a decade, how were they ever going to prove that he did it anyway?

A Gift from Mr Hoey

by Eileen Patterson

Glenortin won't easily forget the Bell Tower Appeal or the death of Francis Henry Hoey.

The money for building the church had run out before any embellishments had been added to the basic four walls and a roof. Generations of local families had happily worshiped and their priests had cheerfully ministered to them without ever feeling the want of a decorative cross or a bell tower. However, on one of the bishop's visits to the glen, he remarked jokingly that the church reminded him of a Presbyterian Meeting House. The parish priest was deeply mortified and within a month set up a committee to investigate ways of raising money for a small tower.

The Hoey household was not even marginally concerned in this. Mr and Mrs Hoey, as a teenage bride and groom, had drifted into the district almost by accident. They were part of a group of travellers who had arrived in the seaside town at the bottom of Glenortin, and when the main party moved on, the Hoeys turned left and decided to put down roots. They followed the river as it bounced among the stones and under the trees and eventually came on a derelict cottage. The youthful Mr Hoey paid the farmer who owned it £500, cash on the nail - the proceeds from some tar macadaming further south - and the cottage was his.

Mr Hoey worked hard and before winter he had a corrugated iron roof in place, the walls whitewashed and the basic necessities of life installed. All winter he was busy indoors and the breadserver reported to all that the "tinkers" were settling in well. Public opinion, expressed in the pub down the hill, was entirely confounded, for it had agreed that travellers could not settle down if they tried.

Small Hoeys made their appearance in due course and grew to be robust in spite of Mrs Hoey's apparent disregard for conventional rules of child-rearing. Their clothing was peculiar and they often went barefoot but when they eventually went to school, they surprised everyone by being intelligent, cheery and articulate. The other children admired them but kept their distance as instructed by their elders.

When he had five children, Mr Hoey quietly walked out of the glen. The social analysts in the public houses had known it was bound to happen. Travellers had itchy feet, couldn't let their backsides rest on a chair. They wondered what Mrs Hoey would do without the breadwinner although they suspected that Mr Hoey had never actually won any bread. He had been known to do some undercover fishing and a little private shooting and trapping, all of which activities would have been punishable offences had anyone of importance known about them. The sensible people of the glen, however, knew that there was enough to go round and anyway none of them was very anxious to be the pot calling the kettle black.

Nobody tried to help Mrs Hoey in her desertion - except the Health Visitor, and Mrs Hoey turned the family's goat on her when she arrived. The school nurse said that the small Hoeys should be taken into care but nobody from officialdom had the temerity to say so to Mrs Hoey.

To everyone's surprise, Mr Hoey came back a year later. He looked no different, no richer, no poorer, and the publican, who had seen him arrive, said he came back with his two hands the one length. He stayed for about three weeks and then departed. This was the pattern of his existence thereafter and it was noted locally that the Hoey family increased in yearly instalments. The schoolteacher, a sarcastic woman, said that Mr Hoey came home annually to welcome his youngest child and to arrange for the arrival of the next. Not that she had anything to complain about. The Hoey's kept her numbers up and each time the Board looked around for a school to close, hers was always spared. Once or twice the priest had tried to talk to Mr Hoey about his parental duty, but the latter was as adept at skipping out of the way of homilies as he apparently was at evading family responsibilities.

Anyway Mrs Hoey didn't seem to mind being a single parent - and a single expectant parent - for most of the year. As the disorganised and unkempt family grew, the older children went off into the world and the younger offspring prepared to follow in their wake. They did return for fleeting visits but the locals couldn't for the life of them tell which was which. In her ramshackle house, Mrs Hoey grew slightly grey but her rosy apple cheeks were unfaded and her good humour unimpaired.

No-one was quite sure how many Hoeys there actually were - although the production line had ground to a halt eleven years before the bell tower appeal. The priest, who had done his duty by perfunctorily baptising each child on arrival, had long lost count and since none of the Hoeys bothered much about the church he didn't worry about it. The schoolteacher swore she had taught fifteen of them but most people thought she was exaggerating. In the pub, people sometimes discussed how Mrs Hoey managed. They knew she never missed a jumble sale and often, as they collected their children from school, they would see their discarded clothing walking past adorning a Hoey child who wore it with panache.

And thus it was down the years.

Then one August evening, eight days before the Bell Tower appeal, the news came that Mr Hoey was dead. The manner of his departure was not clear to the local grapevine but at the final meeting of the fundraising committee, it was generally understood that the remains would be delivered home for burial. The priest was afraid the funeral might cast a blight on the inauguration of the Bell Tower Appeal but, mindful of his duty, he called on Mrs Hoey.

Being aware of the precarious nature of Mrs Hoey's financial situation, he tactfully suggested that she would just be wanting a quiet funeral. He stood in the small hallway and Mrs Hoey, though polite, did not bother to invite him in further. She said she wanted everything decent, and trusted that the priest would do all that was needful in her husband's memory. She said that the neighbours were welcome to call if they wished to pay their respects. He promised that he would tell them and went off to finish his business with the appeal committee.

The whole glen was awash with appeal fever. There was to be a mammoth Fete on Sunday with refreshments, craft stalls, a bouncy castle and a machine that threw people around up and down until they were totally witless. There were to be Ballots and Tombola, a variety of athletic events and even a donkey race. People would be also asked to make a long term commitment to the tower fund and the committee had calculated that four hundred people giving a hundred pounds each during the ensuing year would do the job. The priest said that if a person put £2 into a tin each week, he'd easily have a hundred pounds in a year. The devout members of the committee arranged for the moneyraising to begin with a dedication Mass and the priest liked the idea as he fancied preaching a dramatic sermon. The only cloud on the horizon of the collective excitement was the funeral of Mr Hoey.

On the day of the funeral, it poured. Some of the older members of the community attended, mostly those who remembered the hardworking young husband who had reclaimed the cottage. Other people stood silently in the roadside watching the hearse carry Mr Hoey to the spot from which he would never travel again and some nodded at the other Hoeys who were totally unidentifiable in the downpour. But nobody called at the house to pay their respects. The schoolteacher told the priest that there were so many Hoeys, outsiders would really be in the way. The priest, soaked from standing in the rain (although he had kept it all as brief as possible) went home and had a hot whisky to ward off his death of cold, which he was afraid he had caught.

By Sunday the weather was fine. At five past eleven the road beside the church was crammed with cars and the church crammed with people. Across the road, the appointed guardians of the precious crafts, cakes and competitive games stood in the sunshine smoking while those in the church heard a stirring sermon about Solomon's temple. To give the priest his due, he had worked hard on his sermon and it was a shame he was interrupted in full flight.

The church door opened and the August sunshine exploded down the aisle. Following the sunshine came the full complement of Hoeys - entirely tidy, entirely clean and entirely respectable. There was a kind of glow in Mrs Hoey's face and the younger children looked pleased with themselves. The priest remembered his manners.

"Mrs Hoey! It is very good of you all to come." He waved the schoolchildren in the front row to vacate their seats. The children, who had been brought in procession from the Primary school, started to move, but Mrs Hoey stopped them.

"There's no need, Father," she said. "I just want to say something and then we'll go on home."

"Mrs Hoey, I'm in the middle of a sermon." he told her sternly but she smiled her apple cheeked smile at him and turned to face the stunned congregation.

"Nobody spoke for my Frank at his funeral" she said without rancour. A little wave of shame shivered around the church. "So I'm going to do it now." The priest looked as if he would stop her if he knew how.

"My Frank was a good man. There was nothing more important to him than us and at the beginning we were all right. When children are wee they only need love to thrive. They don't mind what they wear or what they have. But when it comes to making a start in the world they need more. So Frank and me agreed he would go on the road again and every year he came home and brought enough money to see us straight for another year. You all thought it was a queer arrangement but I'd rather be looking forward to something good half the year and remembering it the other half, than living a whole year with a man who would belittle me or ignore me. Frank's been all over, anywhere he could get work, and he put a lot of money in the bank. Every child of ours that left home got their start all right. Josephine and Robert's been to the university and they're solicitors, Jamesie is a teacher and Gerald and Martin has their own shops. Peter's going on for a doctor, Martha and Elizabeth's nurses and there's still enough money for the young ones. Frank has been good to us all!"

In the church, the silence was absolute. Mrs Hoey turned to the priest.

"I hear, Father, you want £100 pounds from everybody for the tower." From her pocket she brought a roll of notes. "There's thirteen of us, counting my Frank, so here's £1,300. But if it was me,

I wouldn't spend it on a tower. I'd give it to some poor children with no father to see to their start in life."

She walked into the aisle and was lost in her children's embraces. They moved quickly to the door and as they went, someone at the back began to clap and then the whole building reverberated with applause.

Actually, Glenortin church never got its tower, but the parish maintains a school for street children in Brazil - to give them, too, a start in life.

Conclusions

by Anne Harris

I call that it is time to go. The child looks up, reluctant. Bends down again.

It is a moon face, pale and round within the confines of an anorak hood. The eyes are a light, almost watery blue. Edgar's eyes in my daughter's face. A constant reminder.

The clothes seem odd - navy blue anorak, cord trousers and a red, hand-knitted jumper, emblazoned with a cartoon character I don't quite recognise. Perhaps it is simply the quality of the knitting that distorts it.

I call again. Again that sombre little face turns its gaze on me. Again bends back to the transporting of the grey sludge that passes for sand in this part of the country. Back and forth, back and forth, clutching the garish plastic bucket and spade bought in a fit of nostalgia, the sludge is carried to the untidy heap that is George's idea of a sandcastle.

No-one has ever taught George how to build a sandcastle, I suppose. Certainly, this is the first trip to the seaside that I can recall in the past four years. But then, I have had only a minimal input into Miss Georgiana Frazer's upbringing.

Not that we come from a deprived background. I may be a single parent, but there have been ski-ing trips, house parties in the country - all the trappings of a comfortable middle class existence. There have simply not been day trips of the traditional kind. George has visited the Hermitage in St. Petersburg but has never built a sandcastle.

I wonder if this self-containment, this sobriety, is normal. I remember my own childhood: being released from the back of my father's Morris Oxford, with its smell of warm leather and the enamel basin my mother insisted we keep in the back seat 'just in case.' Then dashing onto the beach, whooping and yelling. Later, when the sandwiches, gritty with sand, and the warm, slightly over-diluted, orange squash had been devoured, we would run ourselves ragged until it was time to pile back into the car.

Maybe George's life of expensive nannies, progressive nursery schools and tea-parties has been lacking something, after all.

But this is no bright summer's afternoon. It is late September, grey and colder by the minute. The leather of my boots is too delicate, my coat never designed for sitting on damp, chilled rocks.

I call again. My voice competes with the rising wind and the bitter-sad cry of seabirds.

My tone must be more persuasive now. George trudges towards me, the slightly-too-large wellingtons cutting little channels of resentment in the damp sand.

"I want to go home."

"I know, darling." I deliberately misunderstand. "We're going now."

"I mean really home. To my own bed. I want Teddy and Nanny and,

and -" The small face crumples, the bottom lip juts. No tears appear.

It is not natural, this self-containment. No four year old should stifle tears so easily. Another manifestation of Edgar. Though what, in any part of my life, is not?

Thinking of him reminds me of the handful of loose change I have been idly jingling in my pocket, as I sit here, like some travesty of a siren on my rock. Oh that I could be that siren! That I could have the power to lure men with my call. Or call, at least, to one man...

George squelches on ahead, wellingtons caked with grey sand. I follow slowly up the weed strewn, concrete incline that leads to the main street.

Most of the shops have shutters up now. Already they're plastered with tattered fly-posters. The place has an air of abandonment.

I stop at the telephone box on the corner by a neglected little pub. I wonder. Maybe I should try again. Just once more. This will be the last, I promise myself.

The number is so familiar, I could dial it with my eyes closed. Yet, somehow, I cannot seem to get it right. Three times I punch in the number. three times I get wrong.

Suddenly, she is on the other end of the line. Edgar's secretary. His guard dog. My bete noir.

"Who may I say is calling?" I know from the air of disapproval that she knows the answer, yet, obedient, diffident, I give my name. I feel I should apologise to her for my very existence. "Please hold the line."

I hold my breath in trepidation. She knows I'm in a call box. Knows my supply of coins is limited. Is simply delaying until the money runs out.

"Good afternoon." It's Edgar's voice, cold and neutral. "You were instructed not to contact me. I will be in touch when the time is right. Please do not call again. Particularly here." His tone is harshly formal, edged with tightly reined anger. "It really is most inconvenient. I shall accept no more calls."

I stare at the receiver. I've not spoken one word. I've had no opportunity. All my well-rehearsed speeches have dissolved into a hiss of static.

"Mummy! I want to go home!" George is whining, tugging at my coat.

"Yes, darling." I answer, but my mind is elsewhere. I can focus on nothing except Edgar's dismissiveness.

Ten years. Ten years of my life have vanished in the course of a few short weeks.

I was twenty-three when I started working for him. Young, bright, ambitious. I ignored the sniggers, the innuendoes. I would be Edgar Frazer's political researcher. There were no hidden duties in the job-description. I was young, bright, ambitious. I didn't believe the rumours.

I would be different. And I was. For a while. He stayed with me for ten years. I fell in love with him. Had his child.

He wasn't pleased when I told him about the child. Demanded that I get rid of it. Edgar Frazer, the leading anti-abortionist, came to my flat bearing an envelope of cash and a discreet telephone number. He threatened, blustered. Told me he would never see me again.

Then he changed his tune. Cajoled, charmed. Offered me money, promotion. Any price I cared to name.

I named my price. Him. He was appalled. He had known that I was young, bright, ambitious. Had not known that I loved him. That all my aspirations were sublimated to my need. Not for a child. For *his* child.

He relented when the child was born. Came to see us. Was immediately captivated. We were showered with gifts and flowers, myself and my beautiful Georgiana. Everything I could possibly want. Except his love.

Yet my life seemed idyllic. As long as I avoided any thought of his wife, Barbara. His two - no, *their* two growing sons. Only my own life, my own child, counted. I blotted out the rest of the world.

There had been one brief moment of sanity. Or perhaps insanity. He permitted me to name him on the birth certificate. An insignificant act. Except that a journalist, researching an entirely different story, came across the information.

Just one of those tiny coincidences that grow and grow. The beat of a butterfly's wing somewhere in the Amazon and we hear the hurricane. Chaos.

The single shop that is open is brightly lit. A contrast to the drabness of the street outside. We push inside. A bell clangs in the distance.

I have no idea why I have come in. I wander the cramped aisles. Choose things at random: baked beans, bread, drinking chocolate, milk. And paracetamol. A large pack. We'll probably be here for some time.

I have a headache. It's dull, but increasing. Radiating from behind my eyes. Spreading across my crown. Pulsing. Pulsing in time to Edgar's words. *It really is most inconvenient.*

My fingers tighten, knuckles white against the red plastic of the supermarket basket. I want to drop the basket. To scream. Never stop screaming. I want to stamp, shout, remind the world that for ten years - *ten years* - I was convenient.

"Can I have a lollipop, Mummy? Please. Can I, Mummy? Please?"

"Yes! Later!" I must concentrate.

Before I can assert what little authority I possess, the woman at the cash desk holds a sticky red lollipop just out of George's reach. Another decision without reference to me. "What do we say?"

George's lip juts ominously.

I nudge the mutinous little figure beside me. The silence is almost palpable, the lip beginning to tremble. The woman continues to smile but I can feel her condemnation hanging in the air.

I nudge again. "George..." I try to sound assertive.

"George - is that your name? Well, what do you say, George?"

I think I am going to suffocate. Here in this little shop that smells of stale cheese and bacon. I shall just stop breathing. There's no point to my life. I can't even persuade my child to extend a common courtesy.

"Thank you." The sound is almost inaudible as George snatches the lollipop and begins to tear the cellophane from it.

"George. That's a nice name." There's curiosity in the woman's voice, now. I recognise her willingness to trade. Her hostility for my information. For a second, I'm almost tempted. Who else do I have to talk to? I could pour it all out, the whole story to this woman. After all, why shouldn't she claim the reward for finding me, when all the journalists in the country have failed?

There are times when I even consider just ringing the papers. Giving myself up to their questions, to the photographers. I think of Edgar's face if I were to become really inconvenient. But I can't do it. For my own dignity. And for Edgar. Because I love him. Because even now, I still allow myself that tiny glimmer of hope..

As I am about to pay, I grab a couple of tabloids, add them to the basket. The woman's glance is a frank question. I ignore it. Her nosiness is only the normal stock-in-trade of village shopkeepers. She has seen no reason to question the androgynous little figure so eagerly crunching the sweet. We have, at least, passed that test.

It has begun to rain now, sharp little needles carried into my face by the wind. George is grizzling. She's cold and tired. I suppose that I must be, too, yet acknowledging even that depth of feeling would drain what's left of my energy. It's better to remain numb. Better to retain the sense of detachment that has carried me through the past few weeks.

I've been an automation since Edgar's terse phone-call, telling me that the secret was out and that the tabloids were competing for photographs of me and of Georgiana. For all of ten seconds I was elated. At last it was over. All the lies. All the subterfuge.

But Edgar's instinct for self-preservation had already kicked in. His daughter and I may just as well not have existed, except as a threat to his position. His only concern was that, without photographs, they were without proof. So we had to be concealed. Not for our protection. For Edgar's.

I acquiesced. Never thought to question. In the early hours, I hacked off Georgiana's hair with nail scissors, dressed her in garments somehow acquired by the nanny - the only person I felt I could trust - and caught a series of trains to this god-forsaken place. I think we missed the press by minutes.

God. This is the most loathsome, self-catering so-called cottage we could have found. Anywhere. It's a wooden structure, dingy and damp. There's a faint miasma of gas and never, in the time we have been incarcerated here, have I been able to heat it adequately. My God, Edgar. Is this what you want us reduced to?

I heat some baked beans for the child. Try to toast some bread. I'm no cook. Have never needed to be. Yet, surely, even I should be able to manage such a basic meal. But, no. We're surrounded by the eye-watering smell of burnt bread. And by a faint trace of escaping gas. Because the matches are damp and reluctant to light. It makes my head spin.

George eats. I read the papers. It seems there is a price on our heads. One paper is offering a reward for an up-to-date photograph. No doubt, there's someone I once called friend who will oblige. Someone who'll take the thirty pieces of silver.

Both front pages show the same photograph: Edgar's wife. His sons, tall, upright, solemn. And uncannily like their half-sister.

They're walking their dogs - black labradors, naturally. Barbara wears a headscarf, walks with her head slightly downcast. But her look is steadfast. A look that says she has seen it all before. And, I recognise, she has. I am not Edgar's first mistress. Nor, I suddenly realise, will I be his last.

One paper calls her 'Brave Babs.' The other has a banner headline referring to 'Battling Barbara.'

I stare at the pictures. Wonder for the first time about this woman who has lived for nearly thirty years with the man I love. What keeps her tied to such a man? The answer whispers in my mind. *They are married. That is something you can never hope for.*

Inside, both papers also carry the same pictures. One of Edgar leaving a constituency meeting. He is tight-lipped and seems twenty years older than the last time we met.

The other is of me. A grainy, vaguely cruel photograph, taken at a formal event several years ago. I am dressed to kill, bejewelled, holding a glass of champagne. It tells a vicious story.

No matter that it was an unguarded moment. That I don't even wear my hair like that any more. It's a photograph of the ultimate good-time girl.

It's unredeemed by the copy. They are comparing the protrait of a heartless whore with his stoic, long-suffering wife. Another knife in my heart.

I wash up in lukewarm water. I don't know what to do. I no longer recognise Edgar. No longer recognise the woman they tell me is myself.

I look at my hands, slippery with washing-up water. These fingertips have known every inch of Edgar. They hold, in the nerve-endings, the map of his body. My mind knows every nuance of his voice. The velvet of desire. The briskness of business. Now it knows the graveyard breath of his rejection.

George is watching a soap-opera on the flickery little television. I should probably turn it off but I don't have the energy to reach out for the switch.

My mind is oddly blank. I can't even think coherently. All I can hear are Edgar's words yet again. *It really is most inconvenient.*

They stretch out to me. Long tentacles of words. They tighten. Squeeze. My head feels as though it will burst. This headache is almost blinding me. The characters in the soap scream at each other, compounding it, working their way into my pain.

I press my hands to my temples. I want it to stop. All the noise. All the hurt. All the many different kinds of pain.

I know now that Edgar will never come for us. Will never set one fastidious foot inside this unpleasant little building. Will not even try to find us. He is already pulling up the drawbridge that surrounds his life. Already strengthening his own defences. There is no room for me. Or for his daughter.

I fill a pan with milk to make hot chocolate. Georgiana loves it. So do I. Sometimes only that thick, cloying sweetness can penetrate the sourness of life.

I need to take a painkiller. Desperately need to sleep. To escape from this tight band round my head. Yet I can't leave George alone. Alone and unprotected in this strange place. Her father won't come now. There's only me to protect her.

Perhaps if we both sleep. Yes. We shall both sleep. I crush the tablets, mix them with the chocolate, add extra sugar. To kill the bitterness.

We drink it together, curled up against each other on the hard, lumpy little sofa. The characters in the soap kiss and make up.

Georgiana is already asleep. She is beautiful, despite her funny, hacked hair. She doesn't really resemble a boy. People see only what they think is there. Georgiana as a boy. Me, a heartless whore. Only the surface is visible.

The pain is easing now. Not the deep pain inside me. but the tightness in my head is beginning to loosen its grip. I think I shall be able to sleep, after all.

Was there something I should have done? Oh God I wish I could remember...The gas cylinder...Perhaps I should have checked that it was turned off...

I shan't get up just yet. George is so warm here beside me. So warm and comfortable. I shan't disturb her. I'll get up and do it later...Just a little bit later...

Next Stop, America

by Liz Hansford

*H*e leaned forward, a little dark-haired figure tilted out over the edge of the cliff, both his hands reaching as far as he could, fingers and arms outspread, almost flying. His father gripped a big handful of jerkin round his waist, keeping him safe. He grinned through the cold, " Now I'm the nearest person to America in the whole of Ireland, dad, maybe in the whole world."

Every childhood summer it was the same. A westward drive to a caravan park with dank washrooms and a muddy field, or a cottage with no running water, on a remote headland. And then, off in the old, black Austin to Slieve League or Slea Head or the Cliffs of Moher, and one year even out on the ferry to the Aran Islands. He remembered the cliff- top heavy with seething, grey cloud, sea pinks twisted in the wind and his own stomach tight with excitement. Usually they would cross a stretch of bogland, the brackish water lipping over the tops of his shoes, and a ragged stone wall or two, grey-green with lichen; then as they came to the edge of land his father would say the familiar words, "Look Peter! Next stop America." Sometimes it seemed unimaginably remote, others, as if he could feel a certain warmth in the tips of his fingers while the Atlantic winds hustled the rest of his body.

The first few gasps of hot air outside the airport terminal building had shocked him; could he breathe in this place? Water was everywhere: gullies and ditches teeming with alligators; live oaks, their roots swarming into rivers, suspended merely on tendrils; clear, deep rivers with sandy bottoms; Strange how this wetness was so different from home. Water and cold had always gone together in his mind before now.

He rode his way round Disney magic with his grandson, shopped in malls, and watched baseball games, but all the while he longed to get to the Eastern seaboard; to look out over the horizon and say to someone, "Next stop, Ireland," to feel the Atlantic ocean, warm this time; then he would go home satisfied .

For the final week, he headed alone across interstates then country roads, choosing a quiet place right on the North East corner of Florida's coast. Across the board-walk, the beach grasses were dusty dry, but a comfortable warm wind circled him as he kicked through the shell shingle, crushing tellins and milky spirals. Colour-washed, clapperboard houses with wide verandas backed onto the sand, far enough away not to be an intrusion.The stretch of beach was immense, straight as far as the eye could see; he felt the smallness of Ireland in its vastness and his own body conspicuous in all that empty space.Yet it was the same Atlantic ocean, no need to be intimidated. He stood at the water's edge and looked out to sea, way over that wideness was home.

He thought about Kath. River had been her water. As a child she had walked the Lagan tow-path, dipping for spricks to put in jam-jars, tamed into fear of falling in.The whole of their marriage she had heard the old, fierce voices of childhood, the hands grabbing to keep her away from the edge, warning of dreadfull consequences. She must keep everything under control, allow no loose ends of uncertainty. In his love for her, care and caution became the pattern of his life too, until gradually her fears had infected him . Doors were locked and double-checked, routes from A to B carefully mapped and plotted before leaving home - just in case a mistake might be made, instructions on flat-pack furniture fastidiously read before construction, pairs of underpants and socks counted out for the fortnight's holiday in Portstewart; always there was the paralysis of potential disapproval, the fear of getting it wrong clenched tightly around them. Now, on his own, he had chosen safe places: a woodwork class, the community centre, the local bowling club, though he hated the soft-shoed lengths of green, the settled camaraderie.

Far out to sea sharks speared the water - or maybe they were dolphins, but there was no one to ask. And there was certainly no one to talk to about home. A few surfers rode the waves, clusters of families came to swim, but he realised that friendly chat might not be welcome from a middle aged man on his own .

He was fascinated by the brown pelicans; they rode over the beach houses in long lines of lift and flow, moving like a Mexican wave, each dipping down as he reached the same place, falling into a pocket of cool air then rising over the ridge tiles. Occasionally one or two would break away out to sea. They dived sleek, disturbingly close to where he was swimming, and came up with goblet beaks, the water gulching from them in rivulets. As he watched by the water's edge, an older man came by, jovial, dark face smiling, "They'd eat all the fat fish in the sea, don't seem to mind how full they are, always space for more. Bit like me, I guess." His laugh shook through his body.

Peter smiled, "They look a bit like brown umbrellas when they dive."

"Sure do, but there ain't much need of those right now!" And he laughed again. "Enjoy the rest of your day friend, maybe see you again . By the way, Hooky's the name."

Then he was gone, tramping up the beach, canvas jacket flapping. Peter called out his own name but he wasn't sure he'd been heard. He folded his beach towel, sea-horses and fish creased neatly into squares, and went back to the motel.

The next morning Peter bought some extra rolls at the store.

He was in the water when Hooky turned up again, rod and tackle in hand.

"Hooky, 'cos I sure know how to hook 'em in," he explained. "You got to look for the darker patches in the water. You a fisherman? "

"No, just when I was a kid, years ago with my dad."

"You want to learn. Ain't nothin so good as Cajun fish, broiled all black with spices, or Louisiana shrimp gumbo. That's something else."

The rolls seemed feeble but he offered them all the same, sun-warmed from the brown paper bag. "Rolls! These are hoagies. Where you from?"

"Ireland. That's what we call them back home."

He looked out over the sea; memories of cliffs and gulls

levelled against the wind, tides raising the wrack from sandy disarray, green shore crabs and beaded anemones filled his mind.

"Way out there, next stop, Ireland."

"Lot a folks from here seem to go over there, looking for a past. I sure wouldn't find my past there," he laughed. "Got to go a lot further East for that. Any ways, I'm happy 'nough just with the here and now." His voice was deep, like ocean swells rolling the words around.

"I'm kind've looking for a past too, just a childhood dream."

The next day Hooky brought two rods and a rough, wooden crate to sit on. They packed up early evening, five grouper between them.

"You like to come and eat at my place? Don't see how you're going to cook these in some motel room, anyhow, we sure can't divide five fish in two.You wait till you see what Maybelle'll do to these!" The evening passed in warm companionship.The aromatic fish, the hot, sweet-scented peach pie, the strong coffee, the good-humoured chat out on the porch afterwards in the warm night air, made him feel at ease. It was the first time in years that he remembered feeling truly relaxed with folks.

Increasingly the urge to find coves and bays, the desire to be enclosed, left him. He was comfortable on the shore. In the early morning the beach was deserted. Just the pale spider crabs etching the sand with long, delicate claw marks. They sidled across the high-tide line, whitened fingers searching for moisture. When he approached, they disappeared down into the coarse sand. On impulse he started to scrabble down after one, like a kid, scooping and flinging out handfuls of sand. But it was too quick for him, angling downwards, rasping the grit with scuffling claws. He tried another hole with the same results, then another; this time using a firm shell edge to cut into the crab's tunnel. Fast as he went, the crab went faster. Hooky spotted him from up the beach, on hands and knees, tearing at the sand in frustration, bag and towel abandoned way up in the grass.

"You won't get no crab that way! You got to understand 'em.

They're headed down to the water, so you gotta start digging where you reckon they'll come out. It ain't so important where they're coming from as where they're going to. " He picked a spot and they both dug, scraping in alternating rhythm until they saw the white claws reaching into the air. They hauled him out, his legs flailing, trying to reach the safety of underground

"He sure wants to get off-side, Hooky. I wish I'd half that speed!"

"Yeah, but that's the only safe place for him. You and I don't need that amount o'speed, thank the Lord. Wouldn't make it if we did. "

They spent the evening in Singleton's Seafood Shack, surrounded by carved ships and seascapes, and eating the best fish in the world, according to Hooky. He talked of his childhood on Amelia Island, Georgia, his father endlessly moving on to new places to find work.

"This is the first place we've been able to stay and make a living. Though I reckon I can put down roots wherever there's soil. Never got a chance to stay where I was spawned. You been livin' the same place long ?"

"All my life. Same country, same city, near enough same street. It seemed like a sensible thing to do; once."

He thought of all the places still held waiting in his imagination. Key West, where bridges looped and arced through the air, cast like a line, catching the islands till all were hooked and drawn in, taut on steel tension. The Smoky mountains, in the midst of greenness, where the early settlers built cabins and buried their infants in neat graveyard rows. Way out west, to ochre deserts and roadside gas stations a hundred miles apart.

"It's strange, our sense of place in Ireland is kind of dependant on looking backwards, keeping territory safe, mine in particular."

Hooky nodded, "Way I see it, you gotta keep looking forward. Yeah, you can dig in and keep your place safe, but you don't have much of a view."

Peter glanced outside. Over the ocean, the eastern horizon faded in the evening light. Then he turned round, his back to the window.

Dirty Old Man

by Peter Dougherty

*I*t had been a miserable week, cold and wet, a steady drizzle had lain like a sodden shroud over the whole of the town. The skies grey and leaden, a heavy blanket of slothful, deadened indifference.

The botanical gardens were central in the city and the low rumble of afternoon traffic, a constant drone in the middle distance, sometimes punctuated by the muted horn of an impatient driver.

The rain had eased, although the wind, scudding across the open expanse of the garden's central green, would pull arcing lines of fat, gob-like raindrops from the ranks of overhanging sycamore and oak. Whipping across the path below, exploding in puddles gathered in hollows and ruts of the worn tarmac.

An old man came slowly walking along the path, his left foot scuffing close to the ground, his leg a measure of stiffness, not a limp but in no manner as certain as the right. A blackthorn walking stick he carried tapped an accompaniment to each pained pace... silent lips counting. His gaunt face pinched, taut skin stretched over sharp bone. Two days whiskers showed white on his jaw and chin. Skipping rope wisps of hair were brilliantine bonded to his balding pate, ever reddening with the exertion, like a ripening tomato.

His shirt collar was a frayed ruff of soiled, split cotton. Beneath, a yellowing vest showed at the missing top buttons, telling its own story of neglect. The crumpled and stained ancient old raincoat. Shining knees and seat of his trousers completed the picture of years of make-do-and-mend poverty.

The old man kept to the edge of the path, surrendering the crown of the thoroughfare to the speedy and agile. He had learnt to his painful cost, the necessity of having to side step a pumping cyclist, or the horror of freezing in the face of an advancing squadron of young mothers. Engrossed in conversation, pushchairs racing to the fore, chariot like. Their infant pilots, snoozing, oblivious to the havoc wreaked by their maternal siege machines.

The old man paced himself to his first bench on the crest of a rise, threequarters of the day's allotted distance. He called it the Markievicz bench as some teenage vandal had carved the name Markievicz into one of the wooden slats. The spelling had gone awry but he had reasoned what the errant engraver had been attempting. Every day he rested for five minutes before continuing on to the childrens' playground.

He took out his handkerchief and wiped the film of sweat from under his eyes and about his throat. The exercise was an arduous effort, a burning act of endurance that left him sucking air, a dull throbbing in his left calf. The doctors had warned of more operations, his arteries were narrowing and clogged. They viewed his refusal as stubborn, the spite and vindictiveness of senility. Their advice of a healthy lifestyle was fifty years too late. What could they know of old age? What did they know of him? Suffering from the cruellest disease of all... loneliness.

Further along the path he could see the small summer house. Not a proper summer house, rather a sort of partial shelter, the frail structure decayed and dilapidated from neglect, its sad timbers vandalised and graffiti daubed.

Three young men stood by the entrance to the shelter, the old man had seen them there several times before. From his distance he watched as they prowled to and fro, like caged, pacing lions. Bracing limbs against flaking spars, arms raised, wedged onto the lintel. Scuffing stones and staring fiercely. Theirs was an aggression of frustration and resentment. Volatile and unpredictable, like placid dogs that could suddenly turn rabid.

Some days when they had money, he would sit on the Markievicz bench and watch them in their open cage, drinking cheap wine from the bottle. A silent burning anger on their faces...the unmistakable pallor of unemployment.

The old man spat and shook his head at the nothingness of their lives. Only fools believed life was fair. He stood and took the descending path to his right away from the summer house, he was much to old to get entangled with a young man's rage. The biting cold made him shiver, the wind tugged at the collar of his raincoat and he tucked his chin tighter onto his chest. The blackthorn, like a metronome, tapped out a constant to his laboured breathing.

The childrens' playground was a piercing shrill of unrestrained infant shrieks. Immune to the blustering cold, twenty or so youngsters swarmed on and around the swings and roundabouts. At the playground's edge, mothers sat on park benches, gossiping. Babies, swaddled and strapped into pushchairs by their sides.

He shuffled slowly onto the playground. The teenagers at the summer house had forced him to take a longer detour and his allotted five hundred strides were long since past. Pursing his lips and snorting air through his nose, he ignored the blood pounding in his head, the sweat that covered his face. He forced himself to cover the last fifteen yards to an empty bench.

This was the moment he looked forward to each day, his reward. Watching the children at play reminded him of a programme he had seen on the television about otters, their carefree, frolicking abandon and boundless energy. The winter's day brought a translucent shining to their faces, the sharp contrast of the cherry softness of their mouths. The old man envied the children for their youth. He loved them and he hated them. For the time that stretched before them. For what they would have and what he had lost.

He cast a sidelong glance at the next bench along. Two young mothers were deep in conversation. The old man wondered why working class women tried so hard to look alike. Roots showing through bleach, coloured anorak, skintight leggings and baseball boots. Both sucked on cigarettes with the practiced eases of years of experience. He studied them. Still in their twenties, grandmothers in early thirties, old by forty. Snippets of their conversation drifted past.

"Not two year old and she's already sufferin' in bloody silence! Just like a woman."

"Never a truer word. My brood'a boys must've had evry disease a child'll get. Measles! Mumps! Every bloody thing. Not sure who suffers the most, them or me!"

One of the young mothers caught him eavesdropping, abruptly stopped talking and confronted him with a challenging stare. He looked away, not wanting to give offence. It was a pity he thought, something so beautiful would grow to be so hard. Irascibly he got to his feet, banging the blackthorn on the wooden bench. Already the sitting for a while had begun to seize his leg. Slowly he walked to a bench on the far side of the playground. Aggression on the faces of the young women followed him but the old man refused to look.

Seated again, the old man was now closer to the older children. Eight and nine year olds that wanted free of maternal control. Independence they could not yet have, curiosity that was still not theirs to satisfy.

He watched a boy gamely struggle with a bicycle too large for the length of his legs, the boy's face contorted with concentrated effort. The old man smiled at his tenacious perseverance with the unwieldly machine. Like a determined drunk he weaved erratically through the swarming children. Finally losing his battle for control when the bicycle's chain slipped off and freewheeled to a standstill.

In frustration he dumped the powerless machine on the ground and kicked the spinning rear tyre. The boy made a futile attempt at replacing the chain on its cog but without success, it was obvious the mechanics of the bicycle were beyond him.

"Not like that lad, bring it here!"

The boy looked at the gesturing old man, puzzled and unsure of the stranger's offer. His mother had warned him about strangers, especially men. But it was daytime and anyway, she was close by. A quick glance confirmed that his mother was still where he had left her, talking with their neighbour. He picked up the disabled bicycle and trundled it across to the red-faced old man.

"Chain come off?" he asked, stating the obvious.

"I don't know how to fix it."

"What's your name lad?" the old man asked softly, examining the dragging chain.

"Frank," he answered. "That's my brother Michael and Ma's down there with the baby." He added reassuring himself.

"You don't say." The old man looked into the boy's face.

He was aglow with innocence, life poured from his shining eyes. The old man marvelled at his skin, cream and buttermilk, with the faintest hint of strawberry in his cheeks.

"Well Frank, what you have here is a problem of diameters. Do you know what a diameter is?" The boy was baffled. "Small sprocket at the wheel, large one at the pedals. Get your chain on to the smallest cog first, leaves you plenty of slack to tackle your bigger drive at the pedals... see."

The boy beamed as the old man lifted the rear wheel, spun the pedals and the chain slipped back into place.

The boy's confidence and trust gained, the old man patted the bench beside him. "Now young man, I haven't seen you here before, rest your bones there awhile and tell me all about yourself."

At the far end of the playground the two young mothers, absorbed in conversation, were blissfully unaware of the child's new found friendship with the old man.

"I told'im, if he thinks I'm gonna count days'a the month for the next fifteen years, he's got another bloody thing..." She abruptly ceased her tirade against her husband and stared over her friend's shoulder. "Isn't that your Frank?" she said nervously.

"Who's that, do you know'im?"

"I've seen'im hangin' round, watchin' the kids..."

"You don't think...?"

"Better safe than sorry." Both women rose as one.

The old man used his blackthorn as a pointer, detailing to the boy a remedy for the bicycle's chain problem. "Now your drive-chain here is too slack, what you need to do is loosen off this axle lock nut... get your rear wheel back a shade, and Bob's your..."

"Frank! Frank!" One of the young mothers stood twenty yards away and called angrily to her son- "Get here now! Do you hear me!" She stood, hunched forward like a boxer, straining the nylon of her anorax. Lips thin, eyes narrowed.

"Got to go." Frank guiltily pushed the bicycle towards the young woman. As he got closer he sensed he was in trouble. She grabbed him by the arm and shook the boy violently.

"What have I told you about talking to strangers? What have I told you!"

"But he fixed my..." She reinforced her anger with another jolt to Frank's arm. Turning she dragged the boy away. The other young woman gave a last scowl of suspicion at the old man before following.

"You can talk to them till you're blue in the face about men, but it goes in one ear an' out the other!"

"What's he doin' here anyway. They shouldn't allow men in the park durin' the day." The insult was spoken loud enough for all to hear.

Unsteadily the old man got to his feet, tested his weight on his bad leg. He watched as the boy Frank was gruffly led away by his mother. Head bowed, he knew the other women had witnessed the commotion. Humiliated, he slowly began shuffling towards the park gates.

It was a brighter afternoon when the old man made it to his empty bench. As usual the playground was bursting at the seams with children. Like tadpoles in a pond he thought. Propping his blackthorn against the arm of the bench he stretched out his pulsating left leg. Further along the young mothers sat on the same bench as the day before. They eyed him suspiciously.

He watched as the older children played on a climbing frame. A sort of hand over hand monkey swing apparatus that looked frighteningly precarious. The boy with the bicycle from the day before, Frank, was suspended at arm's length, four feet above the ground. He was tiring as he swung from one bar to the next, goaded on by the others, his pride kept him going but the strength was not in the eight year old's arms. It was inevitable he would drop, the twisting awkwardness of his fall to the ground, resounded with a sickening thud that silenced the crowded children.

The hushed, helpless faces alerted mothers to the danger. Instinctively women rushed to the stunned children, a maternal reflex told them something was horribly wrong.

The young mother took one look at her eldest son laying motionless on the ground, a numbing panic swept through her like a shivering paralysis. She dropped to her knees beside the boy, his mouth open, the lids of his eyes half closed.

"Frank! Frank! Oh God no!" She cradled his lolling head in her arms. "Someone get an ambulance, a doctor!"

"It'll be alright love, the hospital's just around the corner, they'll be here in a flash," a woman said with hopeful reassurance.

She clutched the limp boy to her body. "Please let him be alright, please!"

"Let me through, let me pass." The old man pushed his way through the knot of people. With some difficulty he dropped his walking stick and got down on his knees facing the distraught young mother.

"Let me take a look, luv," he said with a confident tenderness. He eased the boy from her reluctant embrace and laid him flat on the ground between them.

Skillfully he administered to the unconscious boy. Lifting a lid he examined an unseeing eye, then felt for a pulse at the boy's throat. The two young women held to each other supportively. Frank's mother's hand clamped over that of her friend, the knuckles showing white, her eyes transfixed on her unconscious son.

The old man held the back of his hand to the boy's mouth, then lowered his cheek to the colourless lips. "Breathing's gone!" Aggressively he went to work on the boy, pulling loose his school tie and ripping apart the shirt.

With two fingers he reached into the boy's mouth and cleared his tongue from the airway. The old man puckered the boy's mouth and pinched closed his nostrils, gently he lowered his mouth over Franks. Powerfully he inflated the lungs, the boy's chest rising and falling.

For what seemed like an age, he pumped air from his own lungs into the boy's body. The old man looked at the lifeless, ashen face of the child, then up at his mother. Quickly averting his eyes, wishing he haddn't, the young woman was a frenzy of panic.

"His lips are blue," a little girl stated with complete detachment. The old man saw the bluish tinge, the cadaverous greyness seeping into his face. He pushed an ear tight on the boy's chest.

"Christ! It's stopped." The young woman screamed and lunged forward. He slapped her across the face, she recoiled into the restraining grasp of her friend. "Keep her back," ordered the old man. "You boy" he snapped at a teenager standing at the back of the crowd. The lad pointed a questioning finger at his own chest.

"Yes you! Get down here now!" commanded the old man, angry at his own failure. The teenager pushed through and tentatively knelt facing the old man.

"Mouth to mouth," ordered the old man. Shock and bewilderment flooded into the teenager's face.

"But I don't..."

"You want him to die!! Pinch his nose closed, form his mouth into an O and blow... Now!!" Time was the only factor, the old man knew he was losing the child's life. He felt for the lowest bone of Frank's chest. Placed the heel of one hand on top of the other and rhythmically began to pump. The child's body convulsed under the pressure. He looked at the teenager, his efforts of mouth to mouth were adequate. Together they worked on the lifeless boy. An ambulance siren in the distance grew louder.

"His finger!" cried a woman. The old man looked at the twitching left hand. The boy's eyelids quivered slightly, he felt for a pulse at the throat, the beat against his fingertips grew stronger. Only then could the old man bring himself to look at the boy's mother. The petrified young woman, slack jawed, eyes bulging, was held in a coma of shock. He nodded reassuringly to her.

"He'll be frightened when he comes round, the first face he should see is you." The mother moved to her son's side as his eyes flickered open, the colour rushing back into his face like a burst of crimson.

"Here's the fellas now," called someone. The ambulance crew came running across the playground, laden with medical equipment.

The old man flicked his head at the awkward teenager. He rose to his feet easily and made to go. The old man waved his hand for assistance, the teenager understood and helped him unsteadily to his feet. The kneeling had numbed his bad leg and the old man stamped several times in an effort to force blood into his foot. As the ambulance crew jostled through the crowd he gave a last look at the frightened boy on the ground, now clutching his mother.

He turned and without so much as a backward glance the old man slowly scuffed his way across the playground, past the empty swings and out of the park.

Not twenty yards onto the embankment when his free arm was suddenly grasped from behind. The old man turned to be confronted by the young mother's friend, who yesterday had wanted to know why he was allowed in the park at all.

She stood there, bleached mop ruffling in the wind, her multicoloured wind cheater straining under her substantial bulk, a chocolate mouthed toddler by one hand.

"Yes luv," he asked cheerily. Her face was puce with embarrassment she was rooted to the spot... a burning mute. He waited. She pulled the toddler closer to her.

"You saved his life," she said, in a barely audible whisper, as if she herself didn't believe it.

He shook his head and smiled. "I just happened to be there, it could've been anybody."

"But... we thought... yesterday... I mean..." She bit her lower lip. He waited. "We thought... you were a dirty old man." She whispered the words like the foulest of confession. The old man reached out and squeezed the young woman's arm in a manner of fatherly understanding. He smiled. "Sure luv, these days... what else can you think." The old man continued on, his foot scuffing the ground, the blackthorn tapping.